This book belongs to:

_____

who loves it very much!

Designer: Celina Carvalho
Production Manager: Colin Hough-Trapp

Library of Congress Cataloging-in-Publication Data:
Finsterbusch, Monika.
Princess Lillifee / by Monika Finsterbusch.
p. cm.

Summary: Having received an invitation to the fairy ball, Princess Lillifee finds
that she has nothing suitable to wear—until her animal friends decide to help.
[1. Princesses–Fiction. 2. Friendship–Fiction. 3. Animals–Fiction.] I. Title.
PZ7.F49856Pri 2006
[E]–dc22

2005027842

Text and illustrations by Monika Finsterbusch
© 2004 Coppenrath Verlag GmbH & Co. KG, Münster, Germany

First published in Germany under the title *Prinzessin Lillifee*
English translation copyright © 2006 Harry N. Abrams, Inc.

Published in 2006 by Abrams Books for Young Readers, an imprint of
Harry N. Abrams, Inc.

Printed and bound in China
10 9 8 7 6 5 4 3 2 1

HNA ▮▮▮▮▮
harry n. abrams, inc.
a subsidiary of La Martinière Groupe
115 West 18th Street
New York, NY 10011
www.hnabooks.com

Princess Lillifee

by Monika Finsterbusch

Abrams Books for Young Readers
New York

Princess Lillifee lived in a beautiful castle. From dawn to dusk, she watched over all her animal friends and tended her flower garden. In the evenings, she would sit on her throne and hear what her friends had done during the day.

One evening, a bird gave her a big, golden letter.

She hurried home to read it. "Hooray!" she exclaimed. "An invitation to my first Fairy Ball!"

That night, Lillifee dreamed of dancing!

The next morning, Lillifee jumped out of bed, ready for the day's tasks. She comforted Clara the mouse, who had hurt herself running away from the cat.

She sang a lullaby to
Pugsy the pig . . .

. . . she tended sick animals . . .

. . . she practiced singing with the birds . . .

. . . she kissed awake the flowers . . .

. . . and she lit the stars in the evening. In fact, she was so busy she forgot all about her invitation to the Fairy Ball.

The following day, Lillifee was painting big colored spots onto Oscar the beetle's back when Clara the mouse found her. "Lillifee, there you are! Are you ready for the Fairy Ball tomorrow evening?"

"Oh, no, the Fairy Ball!" Lillifee exclaimed. "I can't believe I forgot all about it! What should I wear?"

Lillifee and her friends ran back to her castle. "I've got so many nice clothes," she said. "I've got to have a dress in here somewhere."

"I've got it!" Lillifee exclaimed, posing in front of her mirror.

She ran into the garden and called for her friends. "So, what do you think?" she asked.

The animals stared at her. "That's supposed to be a ball dress? Lillifee, you look like a scarecrow!" And they all laughed.

A big tear rolled down Lillifee's cheek. "If I look like a scarecrow, I'd better not go to the Fairy Ball," she sniffed.

"Oh, no," the animals whispered, "what have we done?" They had never seen Lillifee cry before.

"We didn't mean to hurt your feelings, Lillifee," Clara the mouse said. But Lillifee did not hear as she trudged back home.

"We have to help her," Clara said.

"I've got an idea," Pugsy the pig squeaked. All the animals gathered around to hear his plan.

Lillifee's friends met at the lake early the next morning. "Everybody listen up!" Pugsy the pig snorted. "Rabbit, you make the shoes. Hedgehog, ask the magpie to lend us her jewelry, and little frog, you ask the toad for her crown. Mouse and Bear will sew the dress!"

When everything was ready, the animals went in search of Lillifee.

Lillifee couldn't believe her eyes. "Is that for me? Really?" she asked.
"Of course. It's for you to wear to the Fairy Ball!" the animals replied.
"We didn't mean to make you cry."

"We'll help you put everything on," her friends said. When she was finished getting ready, Lillifee turned in a circle so her friends could admire her.

"Now you have to hurry, Lillifee, or you'll be late!"

"How can I thank you?" Lillifee asked.

"That's what friends are for!" they cried as they waved good-bye.

Lillifee heard cheerful music and saw the big, colorfully decorated tent. "What a great gift," Lillifee thought. "Thanks to my friends, I'm going to enjoy my very first Fairy Ball in style!"